THE GREAT DETECTIVE
SHERLOCK HOLMES

— THE DANCING CODE —

THE GREAT DETECTIVE
SHERLOCK HOLMES

— THE DANCING CODE —

The Wife's Fear

"How blessed I am to have you by my side everyday in our morning walks," said the young and handsome Hilton Cubitt to his wife.

"Blessed indeed," said Mrs. Cubitt but her mind seemed to be miles away. Staring pensively at Victoria Harbour, she continued, "There are no mountains in New York, **let alone** a beautiful park like this Peak Garden. It's a real luxury that we get to take walks at the Peak overlooking the sea."

Right at that moment, a gust of wind blew from the seaside, making Mrs. Cubitt's long, golden hair dance in the air.

"My darling, you are always so beautiful when you look out to the sea like this," said Cubitt lovingly to his wife.

pensively (副) 若有所思地、心事重重地   let alone (片語) 更不用說

He could still remember the first time he saw her as though it were yesterday. She looked as beautiful now as she did then. They were on the deck of a **steamship** and she was staring pensively at the *boundless* sea as the sea wind blew *lusciously* through her hair. He was forever *captivated* by her from that moment onwards.

"Oh, you're making me **blush**," said Mrs. Cubitt as she turned around with a **bashful** smile on her face. "My legs are a bit tired. Why don't we sit down and take a rest."

"Of course, my dear." Cubitt took his wife's hand and led her to a bench facing the lawn. This was their daily routine. Every morning after breakfast at seven o'clock, they would

steamship (名) 輪船、郵輪　　boundless (形) 一望無際的
lusciously (副) 迷人地　　captivate(d) (動) 迷倒　　blush (動) 臉紅
bashful (形) 難為情的、害羞的

walk uphill from their house on the mountainside until they reached the Peak Garden. They would walk around the park then sit down on the same bench for a rest before taking the same road downhill to go back home.

Cubitt moved to Hong Kong from London a little over a year ago to take on a new job. Instead of heading directly to Asia, he decided to go to New York first to visit some relatives then take a steamship to Hong Kong from New York. Who would have thought that this solitary journey would forever change his life, for it was on the steamship from New York to Hong Kong that he met his future wife, Elsie, who was also on her own solitary journey. It was love at first sight for the both of them, and they became husband and wife two months after the steamship docked at the port of Hong Kong.

"Elsie, something seems to be troubling you lately. Are you alright, my darling?" Although Cubitt thought his wife was especially beautiful when she was deep in thought, her sadness was starting to worry him.

mountainside (名) 山坡、山腰　　solitary (形) 孤單的、一個人的

"It's nothing…"

"Does it have to do with that letter from America?"

Elsie turned to her husband looking somewhat agitated, "We have a deal. You promised that you won't ask me about my past."

Cubitt swallowed the words at the tip of his tongue and nodded with a sigh, "Yes. I'm so sorry, my darling. I shouldn't have pried." He wished he could say something to cheer her up but he simply could not think of anything to change the subject on the spur of the moment. All he could do was stare at the people doing morning exercises on the lawn in front of them.

Cubitt had learnt from Elsie that Chinese people were in the habit of practicing kung fu in the morning and tai chi was a type of kung fu that was especially popular among the elderly. Cubitt knew nothing about kung fu. He had no idea what type of kung fu moves those people were practicing on the lawn.

As the couple watched the morning kung fu practitioners, Cubitt suddenly heard a low gasp of astonishment from his wife. He turned to her only to see her face drained of all colours, as though she had seen something extremely frightening. Even her lips were quivering incessantly.

"What's wrong, my dear?" asked Cubitt.

"It's…it's nothing…" uttered Elsie uneasily. "I…I'm not feeling too well. I think we should head home."

After saying those words, Elsie stood up and began

kung fu practitioner(s) (名) 練習功夫的人　　gasp (名) 喘氣　astonishment (名) 驚訝
drain(ed) of all colours (習) 臉色變得蒼白　　quiver(ing) (動) 顫抖
incessantly (副) 不停地、不斷地

walking quickly away from the park without looking back once. Although Cubitt did not understand what was going on, he had no choice but to **follow suit**. At that moment, Cubitt was still unaware that an evil force was steadily approaching and would eventually push him to his **fatal doom**.

follow suit (片語) 跟着做　　fatal doom (形+名) 致命的厄運

The Mysterious Stick Figures

"Sheung Wan Hollywood Road please," said Sherlock Holmes in broken Cantonese to the plump **rickshaw** driver after hopping into a rickshaw parked by the roadside. Holmes had just learnt a few **essential** Cantonese phrases from the hotel's doorman.

"Hollywood Road?" repeated the plump rickshaw driver to Holmes while nodding his head. The plump driver then turned to the skinny driver of the rickshaw beside him and said in Cantonese, "The foreigner said they want to go to Sheung Wan Hollywood Road."

"Okay! Got it!" replied the skinny rickshaw driver as he **straightened** his legs quickly with a soft *grunt*. Dr. Watson was sitting in the skinny driver's rickshaw, but the skinny driver was pulling so *effortlessly* as though the combined weight of Watson and the rickshaw was nothing to him.

Not to be **outdone**, the plump driver sprang up right away and began pulling the rickshaw which Holmes was sitting in. The plump driver quickened his steps until he and the skinny driver were running side by side.

rickshaw (名) 人力車　　essential (形) 基本的、必要的　　straighten(ed) (動) 挺直
grunt (名) 咕噥聲　　effortlessly (副) 輕鬆地、亳不費力地
not to be outdone (習) 不甘示弱、不服輸

"Watson, I know that before you came on holiday to Hong Kong, you have decided not to invest in the South African mines," said Holmes to Watson once their rickshaws were running beside each other.

"How could you have known about that?" asked Watson.

"Have I surprised you?" said Holmes with a shrewd chuckle.

"You have surprised me indeed."

"Perhaps you should write down this reply and sign on it."

"Why?"

"Because in about five minutes, you will exclaim, 'That is so simple!'"

"I assure you that I will not utter those words."

"You see, my dear Watson, if one were to present one's  deduction in logical order, like stating each step of the thinking process from ① to ⑥, then it is easy for all to follow," said Holmes lightly. "But if one were to omit the explanation of the middle steps, say ② to ⑤, and just jump directly from ① to ⑥, then people would find the conclusion surprising."

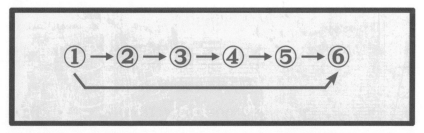

"If you have something to say, please just say it quickly," said Watson to Holmes **impatiently**, wishing his old partner would drop the suspense.

deduction (名) 推論　impatiently (副) 不耐煩地

"Do you remember how you came home very late the night before we left London for Hong Kong? I hadn't gone to bed yet and noticed the start of this *conundrum* ① : there was something between your thumb and index finger on your left hand. From that observation, I made the conclusion ⑥ : you will not invest in the South African mines."

"I don't see the connection between those two things."

"There is seemingly no connection on the surface because I've omitted telling you ② to ⑤ between ① and ⑥." Holmes then began to explain each step of his deduction in logical order to Watson.

conundrum (名) 謎團

14

① The night before we left for Hong Kong, you came home with chalk on your left hand between your thumb and index finger.

② This meant that you just played **billiards**, because a billiards player always daub chalk between the left hand's thumb and index finger in order to **stabilise** the cue stick.

③ This meant that you just met up with Thurston, because you seldom play billiards except when invited by Thurston.

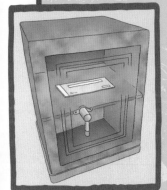

④ You've mentioned that Thurston is considering investing in South African mines and he has asked you to partner with him.

⑤ You don't own a safe box so you keep your chequebook locked in my safe box. You haven't asked me to open the safe box for you recently, which means you have no plans to use large sums of money.

⑥ From that, I know you've decided not to invest in the South African mines.

billiards (名) 桌球　daub (動) 塗抹　stabilise (動) 穩定

"That is so simple!" Watson could not help but exclaim.

Holmes let out a smug chuckle and said, "Didn't I tell you that you will exclaim, 'That is so simple'?"

"Oh, Holmes, you're always finding ways to tease me!" Watson might have sounded annoyed, but deep down he was actually very impressed with his old partner's deduction skills.

As their chatter went on, their rickshaws had reached Hollywood Road in Sheung Wan.

smug (形) 洋洋得意的、沾沾自喜的　　tease (動) 取笑

"We're here," said Watson while pointing towards the building in front of them. "My friend told me in his letter that this hospital is called the Hong Kong College of Medicine for Chinese. It is the first institution where Chinese people can receive western medical treatments. The hospital has just opened and there aren't enough doctors yet. Since my friend has always taken an interest in eastern cultures, he decided to take up on the job offer. My friend is such a lucky chap. Not only has he *landed* an exciting job, he has even met the love of his life, who is now his wife, on the steamship on his way to Hong Kong."

"And this is why you've chosen Hong Kong, the Pearl of the Orient, as our holiday destination this time."

"**Precisely**," said Watson. "My friend just got married, so of course I must come here to congratulate him in person."

chap (名) 傢伙　　land(ed) (動) 找到、得到　　precisely(副) 正是如此

After stepping into the newly built hospital, they quickly found Watson's friend, Hilton Cubitt.

As the old friends exchanged warm greetings with each other, Watson could not help but notice that his friend looked a little glum. Watson asked Cubitt jokingly, "Is everything alright, Hilton? Is work troubling you? Or is your wife keeping such a tight leash on you that you're regretting the marriage?"

"Nothing like that at all," said Cubitt as he shook his head. "It's just that... I've come across something rather bizarre lately and I don't know how I should handle it."

glum (形) 憂鬱的、悶悶不樂的　　keep(ing) a tight leash on someone (習) 嚴格管控某人
bizarre (形) 古怪的

"Something rather bizarre?" asked Holmes curiously. "I just love looking into things that are rather bizarre. Perhaps you can tell me more?"

"Erm..." hesitated Cubitt as he switched his sight from Holmes, whom he had only just met, to his old friend Watson.

"I'm so sorry, Hilton. I wasn't too clear in my introduction of Holmes to you earlier," said Watson as he shot a look of **disapproval** at Holmes. "My travel companion, Holmes, is actually a private detective and being *nosy* is his occupational habit. You don't have to tell him anything if you don't want to. He won't be offended."

disapproval (名) 不滿　nosy (形) 好管閒事的

"Watson, don't you think you're being a bit too straightforward?" *bantered* Holmes lightly.

"But you've only just met Hilton. You can't just pry right into his personal life."

"Actually..." said Cubitt. "I'm troubled over how to solve a difficult problem. Since Mr. Holmes is a detective, perhaps he could help me."

"Always happy to help when help is needed." Holmes shot a shrewd smile at Watson before he asked Cubitt, "So what exactly is the difficult problem?"

"It is this." Cubitt pulled out a strip of paper from his pocket and placed it on the table. "What do you think this means?"

Holmes and Watson *hovered over* 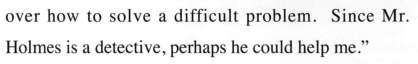 the table for a look. The strip of paper seemed to be **ripped** from a

banter(ed) (動) 開玩笑地說　　hover(ed) over (片語動) 從上面湊過去
rip(ped) (動) 撕開

notebook and on the strip of paper was a drawing of what appeared to be a row of dancing stick figures.

"Looks like a crude drawing. Was this drawn by a child?" asked Watson.

"I'm not sure," said Cubitt as he shook his head before turning to our great detective. "Mr. Holmes, you say you enjoy looking into rather bizarre things. Would you happen to know the meaning of this drawing?"

crude (形) 粗糙的、簡陋的

"It just looks like a group of dancing stick figures at first glance.   What I want to know is why have you taken an interest in this drawing?" asked Holmes.

"To be honest, I don't have the slightest bit of interest in this drawing, but my wife seemed to be extremely frightened as soon as she saw this drawing. She hasn't said anything to me, but I could see the fear in her eyes."

The Unspeakable Past

Holmes pulled out his **magnifying glass** and inspected the strip of paper then said, "There are no invisible words on the paper. The key should lie in the drawing itself."

"Even you can't decipher the drawing?" asked Cubitt.

"It's too early to say right now. I need more time to look into it," said Holmes. "Having more background information would also be of

magnifying glass (名) 放大鏡　　decipher (動) 解讀

immense help in deciphering the images."

"Background information? What do you mean?" asked Cubitt.

"It means we need to know more about your wife," interjected Watson. "Since the frightened one is your wife, we need to know more about her."

"I see. Let me tell you about our story then," said Cubitt. "Before I came here to take up this new post, I first went to New York to visit some relatives then travelled to Hong Kong from New York on a steamship. It was on that steamship journey where I met my wife, Elsie Lee. She told me she bears a Chinese surname because her grandfather was an immigrant from China. The long seafaring journey would've been really dull and boring if I hadn't met Elsie on the ship. We clicked immediately as soon as we met, and we quickly fell in love with each other. I was afraid that I might lose her once we were off the ship, so the day before our ship docked at the port of Hong Kong, I brought up all the courage in me and proposed to her. Elsie is a

immense (形) 極大的   interject(ed) (動) 插話   immigrant (名) 移民

woman with an **adventurous** spirit, and she said yes to my marriage proposal right away. However, she asked me to think it through again carefully before the ship dropped anchor to avoid possible future regrets."

"Why did she say that?" asked Holmes curiously.

"Because she would only agree to marrying me on one condition…" Cubitt took a deep breath before continuing, "She said to me, 'My dear Hilton, you came from a proper family. You are a flawless man, but I'm not a flawless woman. Before I boarded this ship, I was *entangled* with the scums of society. Even though it wasn't by my choice, I still cannot deny my tarnished past. However, I've decided to leave those painful days behind and I don't ever want to talk about my past.'"

---

adventurous (形) 愛冒險的　　flawless (形) 完美的、無缺點的
entangle(d) (動) 糾纏　　scum(s) (名) 混蛋　　tarnished (形) 有污點的

"Hmmm..."

"She went on and said to me, 'Hilton, my love, my past might be tarnished, but I assure you that I have never done anything **immoral** or unlawful. If we were to get married, you will

be marrying a virtuous wife. But you must promise me that you will never ask me about my past, not even once. If you think this promise is too harsh, then we shall part as strangers after we get off the ship and never see each other again.'"

"And you agreed to the promise?" asked Holmes.

"Of course. I love her too much. I know that Elsie is an honest woman and she would never lie to me. I have no reason

not to marry her," said Cubitt. "And I've kept my promise too. I've never asked her about her past.

immoral (形) 不道德的　unlawful (形) 違法的　virtuous (形) 正直的、品行端正的

We were happily married and going about our lives peacefully until..."

"Until this drawing was discovered?" asked Holmes as he waved the strip of paper in his hand.

"No, until a month ago when the first sign of trouble appeared one day in late June," said Cubitt bitterly. "That day, Elsie received a letter from New York and her face was drained of all colours. She burnt the letter straightaway after reading it."

"How did you know that letter was from New York?" asked Holmes.

"The maid brought the letter to me first so I had a good look at the postage stamp."

Miss Elsie Lee
60 Severn Road,
The Peak,
Hong Kong

"Very well. Your attention to detail shall be very helpful in solving this puzzle," praised Holmes. "Did you ask your wife about the content of the letter?"

"No, because I must keep my promise," said Cubitt while shaking his head. "Elsie never brought up the letter so I never asked. But ever since that day, her mind seems to be elsewhere all the time. And she always wears a wary look on her face."

"It's unfortunate that the letter is burnt, otherwise we might be able to find some clues in the letter," said Watson.

"Besides that letter, something else happened about a week ago when we were taking our daily morning walk in the Peak Garden. She was fine at first, but all of a sudden, she was so frightened that she left the park in a hurry."

wary (形) 小心翼翼的、警惕的

"She was frightened all of a sudden?" asked Holmes. "Did she see something scary?"

"The weather was very nice that morning. The wind was blowing gently too. Besides the two of us, there were only a few other people doing morning exercises and practicing kung fu on the lawn as usual, just like every morning," recalled Cubitt.

"Practicing kung fu? What do you mean by that?"

"Kung fu is a form of combat sports of the local people, but it's nothing like boxing; it is more similar to calisthenics instead."

"Calisthenics? What's so special about that then? Why would your wife be so frightened that she needed

calisthenics (名) 健身操、柔軟體操

to leave in a hurry?" muttered the baffled Holmes. "Could she have seen something else that you hadn't noticed?"

"Maybe," said the uncertain Cubitt. "To be honest, I was completely focused on Elsie at the time and I hadn't paid attention to what was going on around us. However, a day later, which was last Tuesday, I discovered a chalk drawing of stick figures by the edge of the windowsill. At first I thought it was a prank by some naughty children nearby, so I just asked the maid to wipe it off. But my wife was very alarmed when I mentioned the drawing to her. She told me if I were to find another similar drawing, she must take a look at it before it is wiped off."

"How is the stick figure drawing on the windowsill

windowsill (名) 窗台、窗沿　　prank (名) 惡作劇

connected to this strip of paper?" asked Holmes.

"Both drawings appear to be exactly the same!" said Cubitt *excitably* .

"Well, that is bizarre indeed." Holmes pondered for a moment then asked, "When was this strip of paper posted to you?"

"This drawing did not come in a letter."

"Then how did it reach you?"

"When the maid handed me a stack of letters three

excitably (副) 激動地

days ago, this strip of paper was sandwiched between the letters. I'm guessing that someone had placed the strip of paper in our letterbox

outside our house," said Cubitt. "I showed the strip of paper to my wife and she fainted right after she saw it."

"Oh dear lord!" Watson was *taken aback*.

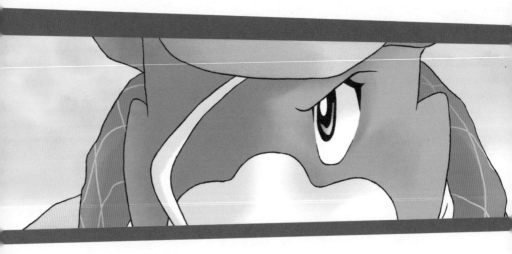

A *frosty* glimmer flashed across Holmes's eyes, "It seems clear to me that the stick figure drawing on this strip of paper must be embedded with some kind of hidden message, and that message must be some sort

---

taken (take) aback (片語動) 嚇一跳　frosty (形) 冰冷的　embed(ded) (動) 暗藏

of threat or blackmail. That's why Mrs. Cubitt was scared out of her wits."

"We should report this threat to the police," suggested Watson. "The police can help investigate who is making the threat."

"I've already reported to the police," said Cubitt with a sigh while shaking his head. "But the police said this looked like nothing but a prank and had refused to open an investigation."

"You can't blame the police, really. The stick figure drawing contains a message that only your wife understands. If she refuses to talk about it, the police have no basis to launch an investigation." Holmes thought for a moment then asked, "Mr. Cubitt, is it really not possible to ask

blackmail (名) 敲詐、勒索　　investigation (名) 調查

your wife to explain the meaning of the drawing?"

"If Elsie were willing to tell me, she would've told me already. I can't force her to tell me. I made a promise before our wedding. I just have to find my own way to get to the bottom of this," said the distressed Cubitt.

"If that's the case, then we shall unravel this together," said Holmes to Cubitt supportively. "I suspect that the stick figures are similar to symbols of a language with its own unique system. Once we figure out the system, we should be able to decipher the meaning of this message."

Stick
figures = Language
            system
↓
Meaning

"Really?" A glimmer of hope shone in Cubitt's eyes

get to the bottom of (片語) 查個水落石出　　unravel (動) 解開

at last.

"A lot more samples must be collected in order to **decode** this unique language system. I need to see more of these stick figure drawings to better analyse the images."

"But I only have this one drawing."

"This much you don't need to worry about. Unless the **tormentor** has given up **terrorising**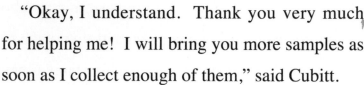 your wife, she should be receiving more stick figure drawings in the coming days," said Holmes with certainty. "Meanwhile, you must pay close attention to your wife's every move. Save all the paper messages with stick figure drawings. And if the stick figures were drawn on a wall, please copy them down."

"Okay, I understand. Thank you very much for helping me! I will bring you more samples as soon as I collect enough of them," said Cubitt.

decode (動) 解讀、破譯　tormentor (名) 折磨者
terrorising (terrorise) (動) 恐嚇、威脅

The Threat of
the Stick Figures

A week had passed since their last meeting with Cubitt. During that week, Holmes and Watson went sightseeing around the city as planned, but our great detective had never forgotten about helping Cubitt. Whenever there was any free time, Holmes would take out the strip of paper and look at it over and over again. Sometimes he would copy the stick figure drawings on his notebook then rip out the page, then copy again and rip out the page again. He would repeat this process many, many times.

On the eighth day, Cubitt came by their hotel just as

Holmes and Watson were about to step out of the hotel. Cubitt looked **frazzled** and restless. Only a few days had passed but Cubitt seemed to have aged years.

"You don't look well, Hilton. Are you alright?" asked Watson worryingly.

"That man came by."

"That man?"

"Elsie's tormenter!" said the distressed Cubitt with **bloodshot** eyes. "I could've caught him but Elsie was in the way. She held onto me and wouldn't let go, then that man got away!"

frazzled (形) 疲累的　　bloodshot (形) 充血的

Holmes and Watson were both taken aback, "How did that happen?"

"It's a long story," sighed Cubitt. "The next morning after I met you, I found a new drawing of stick figures as I was leaving my house for work."

"Was it drawn on paper? Or was it drawn on some other surface?" asked Holmes anxiously.

"It wasn't drawn on paper. This time the stick figures were drawn on the door of the shed. Since our shed is in the back garden near the stone fence, an *intruder* could easily get to it by climbing over the fence. I'm guessing that someone made the chalk drawing on the door in the middle of the night," said Cubitt as he pulled out three pieces of paper from his pocket and handed one to Holmes.

shed (名) 儲物屋/棚　intruder (名) 不速之客、入侵者

Holmes took the piece of paper and counted, "There are eight stick figures in this drawing. You made this copy?"

"You said that the stick figure drawings could contain threatening messages, so I copied every detail very carefully."

"Excellent!" said Holmes enthusiastically. "Then what happened next? Please continue."

"I wiped off the chalk drawing on the shed's door after copying it down, but the next morning, I found a new stick figure drawing on the same door. So I copied that down as well," said Cubitt as he handed Holmes another piece of paper.

enthusiastically (副) 興奮地

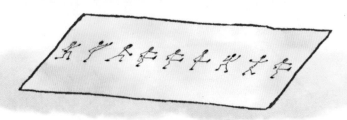

"This drawing has nine stick figures." Holmes took a look at the drawing then asked, "Did you show these drawings to your wife?"

"I didn't want to *rattle* her so I hid them away from her," said Cubitt. "But three days later, the maid discovered a strip of paper drawn with stick figures in our letterbox. The drawing on this strip of paper was exactly the same as the two drawings that I had copied down from the shed's door!"

"Really? Where is that strip of paper? May I take a look please?" asked Holmes anxiously.

rattle (動) 驚動

"Elsie caught sight of the maid handing me the strip of paper. She *frantically* snatched it from my hand, took a quick look then burnt it straightaway," said Cubitt.

"She burnt the drawing?" said Watson. "It must've contained threatening words!"

"My thoughts exactly! This wretched scum is threatening my wife! I must catch this maniac!" said the angry Cubitt. "So I decided to hide in the study and ambush him. I needed to see this monster with my own eyes!"

"Why hide in the study? Can you see the shed from your study?" asked Holmes.

"Yes. My study faces the back garden and it is diagonally across from the shed."

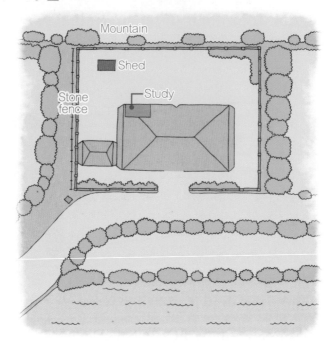

"Were you able to see the man?" asked Watson anxiously.

"Yes, I saw him. In the middle of the night last night at around two o'clock, I saw a black shadow *scurried* towards the shed and stopped in front of the door, as though he was about to write something. So I shouted as loud as I could..."

diagonally across (片語) 斜對面　　scurried (scurry) (動) 匆匆跑過

"Burglar! Help! There's a burglar in the back garden!"

After shouting those words, Cubitt turned around and was about to run out of the study and dash to the back garden, but Elsie suddenly came to the study, blocked the doorway and cried, "Don't go, Hilton! It's too dangerous!"

"But I saw someone in front of the shed! I must catch that man!"

"No! You can't go!" The fearful Elsie continued to block the doorway and refused to step away.

"What are you doing? Let me go!" Cubitt tried to push Elsie away, but Elsie immediately wrapped her arms around Cubitt's body and held tight with all her might, refusing to let go.

wrap(ped) one's arms around (片語) 抱着、抱緊

It took much effort for Cubitt to break free from Elsie's tight grip. By the time he reached the shed, the black shadow was already gone without a trace.

All the shouts and screams had awakened the two housemaids, but they were even slower than Cubitt and did not catch a glimpse of the black shadow by the time they ran into the back garden. Cubitt ordered the maids to search the back garden and other parts of the house, but the intruder was long gone. They did not find anyone hiding anywhere within the vicinity of the large house.

catch a glimpse of (片語) 瞥見　　vicinity (名) 附近、周圍

The Resolute Response

After listening to Cubitt's recollection, Watson asked, "Why did your wife stop you?"

"She wouldn't give me a straight answer when I asked her. She just said that it was very dangerous and she was afraid I would get hurt. I was very angry but there was nothing I could do," said the *dejected* Cubitt. "However, I did discover five new stick figures drawn on the wall of the shed. I've copied them down."

recollection (名) 回憶、憶述　　dejected (形) 沮喪的、垂頭喪氣的

Cubitt handed the last piece of paper to Holmes after saying those words.

"They were drawn on the wall? Didn't you say the shadow was in front of the door? Shouldn't the stick figures be drawn on the door instead?" asked Holmes.

"I am just as baffled as you. Moreover, the stick figures drawn on the door the last two times were only as tall as a finger, but this time they were larger than my hand."

"That is pretty large."

"Yes, as though the drawer needed to make sure that no one would miss the drawing."

"Needed to make sure that no one would miss the drawing... Hmmm..." Holmes muttered to himself as he pondered for a moment before asking, "The wall where you found the stick figures, which direction does it face?"

"My house is built against the mountain. The shed is in the back garden and that wall faces a small mountain <u>slope</u>."

"What's on the small mountain slope?"

"There's a road with <u>railings</u> on the small mountain slope."

"If someone were to stand on that slope, could he or she see that wall of the shed?"

Cubitt gave Holmes a look of **puzzlement**, as though he did not understand the meaning of

---

slope (名) 斜坡　railing(s) (名) 欄杆、圍欄　puzzlement (名) 困惑、費解

Holmes's question.

"Perhaps the drawer of those five large stick figures was not the black shadow you saw by the shed's door but someone else instead," said Holmes as a frosty glimmer flashed across his eyes.

"What do you mean?" asked Cubitt.

"You still don't understand? Those five large stick figures were drawn by someone from your house!"

"What?" Both Cubitt and Watson were greatly taken aback.

"What makes you say that?" asked Watson.

"Try comparing the stick figure drawings on the door and the new drawing on the wall, and you would come up with the same conclusion too." Holmes then listed the details of the comparison.

Stick Figures on the Door	Stick Figures on the Wall
①The size was only as tall as a finger. The drawer was not worried that the intended **recipient** of the message could not see the drawings, so there was no need to draw them big.	①The size was larger than a hand. The drawer was worried that the intended recipient of the message might not see the drawing, so there was a need to draw them big.
②The door faces the house. The drawings were meant to be seen by someone in the house. That's why they were drawn on the door that faces the house.	②The wall faces the road on the small mountain slope. The drawing was meant to be seen by someone outside the house. That's why the stick figures were drawn on the wall that faces the road on the small mountain slope.
③One drawing had eight stick figures and the other had nine stick figures. The drawer needed to **convey** his intention clearly so the messages were longer.	③There were only five stick figures. The drawer was only replying to the stick figure drawings on the door. There was no need for the message to be long.

"Hence, I believe the five stick figures on the wall were drawn by someone in the house. And that person is none other than Mrs. Cubitt!" said Holmes **without reservations**, **hitting the nail on the head**.

recipient (名) 接收人、收件人　convey (動) 傳達
without reservations (片語) 毫無保留地、毫不猶豫地
hit(ting) the nail on the head (習) 斬釘截鐵、一針見血

"Oh my God…" Cubitt was stunned speechless.

"That makes sense," agreed Watson with his old partner's deduction. "From Mrs. Cubitt's frightened reaction, the stick figures on the door were meant for her to see. And if those five stick figures on the wall were a reply to those drawings on the door, then the replier must be Mrs. Cubitt."

"Precisely," said Holmes. "Moreover, that message on the wall was so short that I can sense how **resolute** she was in her reply."

"Why do you say that?" asked Cubitt.

"Very simple," analysed Holmes. "There are usually four different responses when a person is being issued with a threat : **A** **ignore** it, **B** accept it, **C** refuse to accept it, **D** try to **negotiate** ."

---

resolute (形) 堅決的、堅定的　　ignore (動) 不理會、無視　　negotiate (動) 談判

"If the five large stick figures were drawn by Mrs. Cubitt, then it certainly isn't **A**," said Watson.

"That's right," said Holmes. "And it isn't **D** either, because if Mrs. Cubitt had wished to negotiate, the message would've been longer and not just a short message of five stick figures.

"What about **B**?" Cubitt asked worryingly. "Has she accepted the threat? Is that why her reply was so short?"

"It's possible, though I don't think that's the case here," deduced Holmes. "If she had accepted the threat, she could just get in touch with the *intimidator*

---

intimidator (名) 威嚇者

directly instead of drawing stick figures to issue her reply."

"Not necessarily," disagreed Watson. "Maybe she doesn't know how to get in touch with the intimidator so she drew the stick figures to request a meeting."

"If that's the case, then the message would need to be longer, just like **D**. Drawing only five stick figures may not be enough to convey that intention clearly," said Holmes.

"So this leaves only **C**. She refuses to accept the threat," said the slightly relieved Cubitt. "I'm glad that Elsie is refusing to accept the threat. At least I know we're on the same side and we can stand up to her tormentor together."

"Yes," said Holmes. "From all the clues that we have gathered so far, it seems like Mrs. Cubitt not only knows how to decipher those stick figures, she also knows how to use those stick figures to convey messages. Moreover, she knows that this intimidator is far from being a gentleman. She knows that direct *confrontation* would only lead to grave danger. However, something must be holding back the intimidator. He has chosen to convey his messages by drawing stick figures, which means he needs to make sure that no one else other than Mrs. Cubitt knows about his identity and the meaning of those stick figures. Otherwise, he could've chosen a less **convoluted** way to threaten Mrs. Cubitt."

confrontation (名) 對抗、衝突　grave (形) 嚴重的、嚴峻的
convoluted (形) 複雜的、迂迴的

"I don't care who he is! I must put a stop to this!" said the angry Cubitt bitterly.

"How will you go about doing that?" asked Watson.

"I will hire a few big, strong fellows and have them hide in the garden. They will **ambush** that creep when he shows up again and give him a good beating. He won't dare to *harass* Elsie again after that!"

"You absolutely must not do that!" cautioned Holmes. "Didn't you hear what I just said? This intimidator is dangerous. The fact that your wife had stopped you from chasing after him is proof. I think you should direct your focus on doing all that you

ambush (動) 伏擊　　creep (名) 壞蛋、討厭的人　　harass (動) 騷擾

54

can to protect yourself and your wife instead."

"What should I do then? I can't just sit around and wait for the worst to happen."

"Please give me one more day," said Holmes. "There should be enough material now for me to conduct a more thorough analysis. I should be able to crack the hidden messages in the stick figure drawings within a day. After that, we should be able to figure out the identity of the intimidator and ask the police to arrest him."

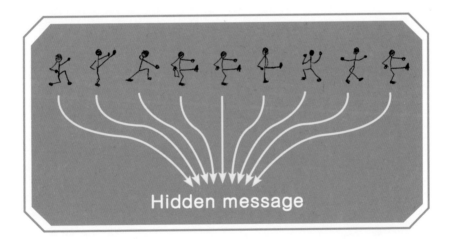

"One day?" muttered Cubitt as he thought over Holmes's words. "Alright, I will wait one more day."

crack (動) 拆解、破解

"Please leave me all of the stick figure drawings."

Cubitt agreed with a nod.

"Remember, you must protect your wife and don't try anything **reckless**. You should go back home now and wait for my good news," reminded Holmes.

"Okay, I understand." After thanking Holmes and Watson, Cubitt headed back home.

reckless (形) 輕舉妄動的、魯莽的

The Coded Message

"Your friend seems rather **stubborn**," said Holmes worryingly. "I hope he listens to me and doesn't try anything reckless."

"He is a <u>righteous</u> man who **abhors** evil, and right now his own wife is being threatened. His fury is only understandable." Watson then changed the subject and asked, "So you're confident that you can decode the stick figure drawings within a day?"

stubborn (形) 固執的　　righteous (形) 正直的、正義的　　abhor(s) (動) 痛恨

Holmes let out a shrewd chuckle and said, "Actually, I've already figured out the angle of approach in decoding the stick figures while we were sightseeing around the city the past few days. I just didn't have enough material at that time to completely crack the code yet."

Upon saying those words, Holmes spread out all the stick figure drawings on the table and immediately **dived into** the decoding work. Watson knew better than to disturb Holmes, so he sat down on a chair near the table and watched on quietly.

Holmes stood by the table and stared at the drawings without moving a muscle. An hour had passed before he

dive(d) into (片語動) 埋頭於、投入

finally reached for the hotel's stationary drawer to take out a few sheets of paper. He then cut the sheets of paper into small squares and wrote down each of the 26 letters of the alphabet on the individual squares.

Could each of the stick figure represent a letter of the alphabet? thought Watson.

Watson watched as his old partner placed the alphabet squares below the paper strips of stick figure drawings. Holmes lined the squares into a row and began to make words with the squares. Holmes would

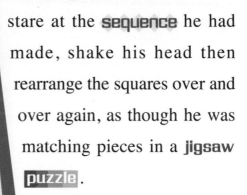

stare at the **sequence** he had made, shake his head then rearrange the squares over and over again, as though he was matching pieces in a **jigsaw puzzle**.

Whenever Holmes was happy with a particular sequence, he would let out a light whistle of satisfaction. But whenever he was **stuck**, he would stare hard at the alphabet squares with

sequence (名) 排列   jigsaw puzzle (名) 拼圖遊戲   stuck (形) 想不通的

his eyebrows tightly **furrowed**.

"How is it? Are you able to crack it?" Watson could not stay quiet any longer.

Holmes *shushed* Watson with a wave of his hand. He then walked to the window and looked out to the streets. Holmes was so **absorbed** that an hour had passed before he was finally tired of looking out the window and began pacing around the hotel room. Sometimes he would take out his pipe for a few **puffs**. Sometimes he would rub his hands then sit down at the table again and resume playing the **perplexing** word-building game with the alphabet squares.

"Aha! I've got it at last!" said Holmes excitedly to Watson when the sun had already begun to set.

furrowed (形) 緊皺的　　shush(ed) (動) 示意某人安靜下來　　absorbed (形) 專注的
puff(s) (名) 吸一口煙　　perplexing (形) 令人費解的

"Have you successfully decoded the stick figure drawings?" responded Watson with equal excitement.

"Yes, I've cracked it, but I must go out now to send a telegram. Please enjoy your supper without me." Holmes walked out of the room right after saying those words. He left the hotel so quickly that Watson did not even have a chance to ask for details.

He is like this every time! Always keeping me in the dark at key moments and leaving me in suspense all by myself! thought Watson as he rolled his eyes in frustration.

It was already late evening by the time Holmes returned to the hotel.

"It's pretty late. Where have you been?" asked Watson.

"I went to send a telegram."

"But sending a telegram doesn't take that long."

"No, it doesn't take much time to send a telegram but it takes a long time to wait for a reply," said Holmes. "I waited for three hours before I received a reply."

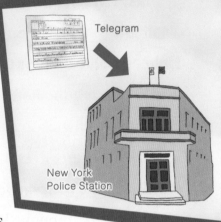

Telegram

New York Police Station

"Whose reply were you waiting for?" asked the curious Watson.

"The police station in New York."

"What? New York Police Station?" asked the surprised Watson. "Is this case connected to criminals in New York?"

"Oh yes, there is a very important connection," said Holmes with a shrewd chuckle. "After I received the reply, I went over to the Central Police Station and asked an acquaintance of mine to conduct an investigation."

acquaintance (名) 認識的人、熟人

"You have acquaintances in Hong Kong?" asked the surprised Watson.

"Yes. You know him too, actually."

"I do? Who is he?"

"Superintendent Teigen. He asked to transfer to Hong Kong after working on that kidnapping case. It seems like he is pretty happy working in Hong Kong."

"Oh, Teigen! I remember him. It's good to have acquaintances close by. So did you find what you were looking for?"

Holmes let out a huge yawn and waved his hand, "Yes, but I've been **bustling** about and I'm very tired. I don't want to talk now. We shall go visit Cubitt first thing tomorrow morning and tell him about the investigation results. I'll **divulge** all the details at one go. Right now, please let me sleep. Goodnight." On

---

superintendent (名) 警司　　bustling (bustle) (動) 忙着、奔波　　divulge (動) 透露

that note, Holmes *plopped down* on the bed, leaving the **dumbfounded** Watson standing by himself in the middle of the room.

*Holmes is **keeping me in suspense** again! He must be doing this on purpose to **drive me up the wall**! Oh how I just really hate him sometimes!* thought the frustrated Watson.

Holmes and Watson woke up early next morning after a good night sleep. They quickly washed up and were about to head downstairs to the breakfast room. As Holmes reached for the doorknob of their hotel room's front door, he noticed a letter was on the floor near the door.

From: Hilton Cubitt
To: Mr. Sherlock Holmes

"There's a letter on the floor. The hotel staff must've slipped the letter under the door last night without

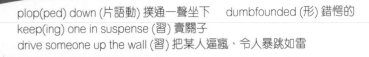

plop(ped) down (片語動) 撲通一聲坐下　　dumbfounded (形) 錯愕的
keep(ing) one in suspense (習) 賣關子
drive someone up the wall (習) 把某人逼瘋、令人暴跳如雷

64

waking us up," said Holmes as he picked up the letter for a look. "It's from Cubitt. He must've sent someone to deliver the letter to us."

"Bringing us a letter so late at night? It must be something very urgent," said Watson with an uneasy feeling.

Holmes's eyebrows furrowed in concern upon hearing Watson's words. He immediately opened the letter for a look.

Dear Mr. Holmes,

Sorry to be bothering you so late at night. At around 10 o'clock this evening, one of my maids found a paper aeroplane in the back garden. She unfolded the piece of paper for a look and saw two rows of stick figures drawn on the paper. When the maid showed the drawing to me and my wife, my wife was so frightened that she sobbed hysterically in her hands, yet she still refused to open up and reveal the truth. I could tell from my wife's reaction that the message this time was much more alarming than before, so I am delivering the paper aeroplane to you right away. Please take a look and see if you can decipher the meaning of these stick figures.

Sincerely,
Hilton Cubitt

hysterically (副) 歇斯底里地

"Here is the paper aeroplane," said Holmes as he **cringed** his **eyebrows**. "It seems to carry a strange **odour**."

"Really?" said Watson, giving the paper aeroplane a sniff. "You're right. It does smell strange. What could it be?"

"That's not important now. Let's take a look at the content first." Putting aside the strange odour for now, Holmes quickly unfolded the paper aeroplane for a look.

"The first stick figure is E... The second is L... The third is S... The fourth is I... The fifth is E... That spells ELSIE." Holmes was muttering to himself aloud, but his muttering soon turned into silent movements of his lips.

However, Holmes suddenly began to mutter aloud again when he reached the end of the message, "The twenty-second is

cringe(d) eyebrows (動＋名) 皺眉　　odour (名) 氣味

66

G… The twenty-third is O… The twenty-fourth is D…
That spells GOD!"

"God? What does that mean?" asked the baffled
Watson.

"Oh no! This is really bad!" shouted Holmes all of
a sudden. "We must head to Cubitt's home right now
before it's too late!"

Meet Thy God!

When Holmes and Watson reached Cubitt's home in Mid-Levels, two policemen in uniform were already standing guard in front of the entrance. Watson had a sinking feeling, but all he could do was pray in silence that nothing serious had happened to his friend.

sinking feeling (習) 不祥的預感

"Is Superintendent Teigen inside? If so, please tell him that Sherlock Holmes is here," said Holmes to the policemen at the front door.

Soon after one of the policemen went inside to pass the message, the tall police superintendent named Teigen came outside to greet Holmes and Watson, "You came just in time. I was about to send someone for you."

"Why? Has something horrible happened?" asked Holmes worryingly.

"Very horrible indeed," said Teigen as he shook his head. "One dead and one gravely injured."

"Oh no!" exclaimed Watson in astonishment.

"Don't tell me that…the dead one is Mr. Cubitt?" asked Holmes nervously.

"It is Mr. Cubitt, unfortunately. He died of a gunshot wound to the heart."

Both Holmes and Watson were greatly taken aback after hearing those words.

Holmes let out a deep sigh, "What a regrettable twist of fate ! If only the hotel staff had woken us up last night to give us the letter, this bloodshed could've been avoided."

"What are you talking about?" asked the confused Teigen.

Holmes told Teigen in detail about the letter he found by their hotel room door this morning. Holmes further explained, "A paper aeroplane with a drawing of 24 stick figures was included in the letter. Those stick figures actually spelled out 'ELSIE, PREPARE TO MEET THY GOD'."

=ELSIE PREPARE
=TO MEET THY GOD

twist of fate (習) 造物弄人、命運無常　　bloodshed (名) 流血事件

"Good heavens! Is that the meaning of those stick figures?" asked the *overwhelmed* Watson.

"That's very odd," said the baffled Teigen. "If what you've just told me were true, then it means someone out there wants to harm Mrs. Cubitt. So why is she the killer?"

"What? Mr. Cubitt was killed by Mrs. Cubitt?" Holmes and Watson could not believe their ears.

"That's what I've gathered from the two maids who were in their bedrooms upstairs when they heard two gunshots. The maids said they went downstairs for a look right after hearing the loud noises and found Mr. Cubitt already dead and Mrs. Cubitt lying on the floor barely breathing. Since Mr. and Mrs. Cubitt were **quarrelling** quite often lately, the maids think it's possible that Mrs. Cubitt shot her husband then took the gun to herself."

Watson challenged the **notion** right away, "From what I know, Mr. and Mrs. Cubitt were a loving couple. I don't think Mrs. Cubitt would get so **infuriated** over a quarrel that she would **pull a trigger** on her husband."

---

overwhelmed (形) 不知所措的、不可置信的　quarrel(ling) (動) 爭吵
notion (名) 看法　infuriate(d) (動) 憤怒　pull a trigger (動+名) 開槍

"Is that so?" wondered Teigen as he gave Watson a **sceptical** look. "Have you ever met Mrs. Cubitt before? Do you know her well?"

"Well......" Watson was at a loss for words.

"Obviously, we can't just take the word of the maids' **one-sided account** ," said Teigen. "However, we did find a **manila envelope** with US$500 inside on the floor of the study. Maybe the couple was quarrelling over money issues, otherwise how would you explain that envelope of money? Also, according to the doctor who rushed over to treat the Cubitts, Mrs. Cubitt's wound is on her left **temple** and the bullet is still inside her head. *Remnants* of **gunpowder soot** are found on her left sleeve and traces of blood are found on the <u>gun barrel</u>. So without

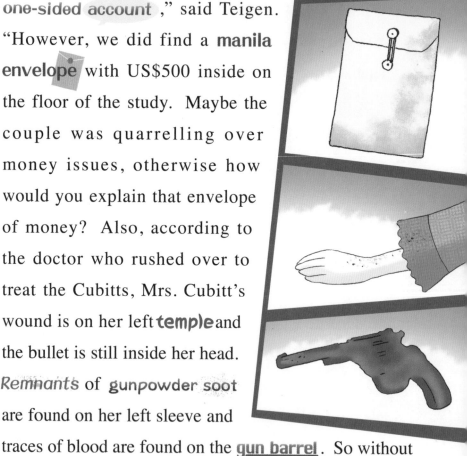

---

sceptical (形) 懷疑的   one-sided account （片語）片面之詞、單方面的證詞
manila envelope (名) 公文袋   temple (名) 太陽穴   remnant(s) (名) 殘留物
gunpowder soot (名) 火藥灰   gun barrel (名) 槍管

72

a doubt, the wound is caused by a close range gunshot."

Holmes thought for a moment then asked, "Has Mrs. Cubitt been sent to the hospital yet? Is Mr. Cubitt's body still here?"

"We moved the body away already," said Teigen. "The manila envelope filled with US dollars and the

revolver with four remaining bullets have also been taken away, but the rest of the crime scene is untouched. Would you like to take a look?"

Teigen was already leading the way into the mansion before Holmes could offer his reply. After walking through a long **hallway**, the three men came to the study that faced the back garden.

As soon as he stepped into the study, Watson could see two human-shaped **chalk outlines** drawn on the floor. One chalk outline was near the window and the other one was at the centre of the room. There were also two other chalk outlines indicating that the manila envelope was found near the window and the revolver was found between the two human-shaped chalk outlines.

"Which outline is Mr. Cubitt?" asked Holmes.

"The one at the centre," said Teigen as he pointed at

the chalk outline on the floor. "No soot remnants were found on his wound, which meant he wasn't shot from close range. The fact that the revolver was found on the floor between Mr. and Mrs. Cubitt meant the maids' speculation could be true, that Mrs. Cubitt shot herself in the head out of guilt after shooting her husband to death. When she fell down, the revolver dropped on the floor between them. According to the maids, Mrs. Cubitt was left-handed, so finding the revolver near her left hand fits the picture."

As Holmes listened to Teigen, Holmes carefully walked around the chalk outlines then towards the tightly shut window. He raised his head to check above the window then lowered his head to inspect below the window. He then looked through the window at the scenery outside and pointed at a small brick house in the back garden, "Watson, I think that's the shed that Mr. Cubitt had talked about."

speculation (名) 推測   brick house (名) 磚屋

"Yes…" Watson recalled how Cubitt told them about the stick figure drawings found on the door and wall of the shed.

"Was this window shut during the shooting?" Holmes asked Teigen.

"The maids said they hadn't touched the window, so the window should be shut all this time."

"What were the Cubitts wearing? Were they in their pyjamas?"

"Yes, they were wearing pyjamas."

pyjamas (名) 睡衣

Holmes pondered for a moment then asked, "Where are those two maids now?"

"They're upstairs," said Teigen as he pointed his finger upwards. "I've asked them to stay put in their rooms."

"Can I interview them?"

"Of course. I'll ask them to come down."

"No, let's go upstairs," said Holmes. "I want to take a look around on my way up."

Watson knew well that Holmes was always in the habit of inspecting not only the crime scene but also the **surroundings** whenever possible. Moreover, since the two maids had run from their rooms upstairs to the study downstairs, the distance between their rooms upstairs to the study, the loudness of the gunshots as well as the amount of time it took to dash to the study were all important factors of consideration.

Divided along the two sides of the upstairs corridor

stay put (習) 留在原地　　surroundings (名) 周圍　　loudness (名) 音量

78

were eight rooms. Four rooms faced the mountainside and the other four rooms faced the seaside . The Cubitts' bedroom and the maids' bedrooms all faced the seaside on the opposite ends of the corridor. Teigen had already checked and confirmed that besides these three rooms, the other five were unoccupied guestrooms, and their doors and windows were firmly shut. All of the windows and doors downstairs were also shut. And there were no signs of breaking and entering.

Facing Mountainside ↑

Guestroom	Guestroom	Guestroom	Guestroom
Corridor			
Maid Mrs. King's Bedroom	Maid Saunders's Bedroom	Guestroom	The Cubitts' Bedroom

Facing Seaside ↓

Teigen led Holmes and Watson to take a look at the Cubitts' bedroom before walking to the maids' bedrooms. The first maid they interviewed was a young woman named Saunders. She was apparently still very **shaken up**, because her face was pale as ghost.

seaside (名) 海邊、海濱   shake(n) up (片語動) 心神不定、受驚過度

The Secret of the Window

"How did you know something was happening downstairs? And what time was it then?" asked Holmes right away after a brief introduction of himself to the maid named Saunders.

"I heard noises... I was awakened by a loud bang... I **shot up** from my bed and looked at the clock. It was around three o'clock in the morning," recalled Saunders in a trembling voice. "I didn't know what was

shot (shoot) up (片語動) 嚇得彈起來   trembling (形) 顫抖的

happening, so I quickly put on my robe to go for a look."

"What happened after?" asked Holmes.

"I had just finished putting on my robe when I heard another loud bang, but it didn't seem to be as loud as the first one. I was so startled that I ran out of my room immediately. That's when I saw Mrs. King had also run out of her room with a candle in her hand."

"Then the two of you went downstairs?"

"No. We first went to Mr. and Mrs. Cubitt's bedroom," said Saunders. "We were very frightened…so the first thing we thought of…was to find Mr. Cubitt."

"So you walked to the other end of the corridor and knocked on the Cubitts' bedroom door?"

"No… The door was open… We didn't need to knock to see that the room was empty…"

robe (名) 長袍

"The door was open?" asked Holmes. "What about the window? Was the seaside-facing window left open?"

"The window...? The window should be open... The weather has been rather

hot lately. Mrs. King and I have also been leaving our windows open when we go to sleep at night."

"What about the windows downstairs?"

"Downstairs? Those were definitely shut," said Saunders with certainty. "Mr. Cubitt had told us repeatedly to make sure that all the doors and windows downstairs must be tightly shut at night before going to bed, since intruders have been coming into the back garden lately."

Why is Holmes so concerned about the doors and windows? Could there be some hidden clues that might help solve the case? wondered Watson. Standing near Holmes with his eyebrows furrowed, Teigen also had no idea what our great detective **had up** his **sleeve** .

"Very well," nodded Holmes, seemingly satisfied with Saunders's answer. He then resumed his questioning, "What did you and Mrs. King do when you couldn't find the Cubitts in their bedroom?"

"Mrs. King and I then…"

"Sorry, but…" Holmes suddenly interrupted Saunders and asked instead, "Before you went downstairs, did you remember smelling any unusual odours?"

Watson knew well that this was a questioning technique that his old partner liked to use. Sometimes

had (have) up one's sleeve (習) 胡蘆裏賣甚麼藥、袖裏乾坤

when an interview reached a key point, Holmes would ask an unrelated question to **throw off** the interviewee, giving the interviewee no time to come up with lies to answer the unexpected question.

"Odour?" Saunders thought for a moment before continuing, "I do remember smelling the scent of gunpowder."

"Are you sure? I meant before you went downstairs, not after."

"Yes, I am sure. I could smell it right away as soon as I stepped out of my room, actually."

"Very well," nodded Holmes again. "Where did you go first after you headed downstairs?"

"The study was near the bottom of the staircase, so we went to the study first."

"Did you knock before you went in?"

"No. The study's door was open. We walked in without knocking on the door." At this point, Saunders suddenly began to choke on her sobs. "We... We saw..."

---

throw off (片語動) 打斷、混淆   choke (動) 喘不過氣來、哽咽

"It's alright. You don't need to carry on." Holmes gave her shoulders a consoling pat and said, "Thank you very much for your help. You should take some rest."

After his interview with Saunders, Holmes went to Mrs. King's room and asked Mrs. King the same questions. Upon confirming that Mrs. King's answers were no different to Saunders's, Holmes appeared to *have a firm grasp* of the situation. He said to Teigen,

consoling (形) 安慰的   pat (名) 輕拍
have a firm grasp (習) 很有把握、胸有成竹

"That's enough questioning. Let's go back to the study."

When the three men returned to the study, Watson asked Holmes, "Why didn't you ask the maids about what happened after they came into the study? Isn't that more important?"

Teigen glanced over to Holmes, wondering the same as Watson.

"Don't you get it?" said Holmes as he looked around the study. "As long as this room hasn't been **tampered with**, we can pretty much imagine what they've seen. The maids would only break down in tears of misery if I were to keep questioning. Besides, I've already obtained the confirmation of a very important detail —— the scent of gunpowder."

"What's so curious about that? Firing a gun always leaves a trail of gunpowder odour."

"The curious part is that both Saunders and Mrs. King could smell the gunpowder odour upstairs as soon as they opened their bedroom doors."

tamper(ed) with (片語動) 蓄意破壞

"You know very well that odour travels through air. There's nothing unusual about it," said Watson.

"No…" Teigen rubbed his chin and said, "If the air weren't moving, the odour 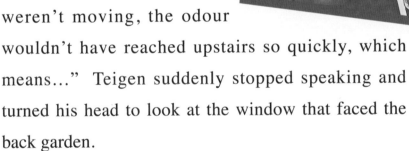 wouldn't have reached upstairs so quickly, which means…" Teigen suddenly stopped speaking and turned his head to look at the window that faced the back garden.

"Precisely!" Holmes extended his arm and pointed his index finger towards the window, "It means that the study's window must've been open during the shooting!"

"Oh I see!" Watson finally understood the logic. "You're saying that because that window was open, wind blew through that window into the study, then the gunpowder odour was carried in the wind through the study's door to upstairs."

"Precisely!" said Holmes. "Since the two maids had left the windows in their bedrooms open, and all the other windows and doors in the house were shut, the gunpowder odour had nowhere to go but upstairs towards their rooms due to *air convection*. That's why they could smell gunpowder right away as soon as they opened their bedroom doors."

air convection (名) 空氣對流

Looking at the nearby mountain through the window, Watson thought, *But this window is facing the mountain and not the seaside. And that mountain is like a huge* shield *blocking the wind. How could Holmes be so sure that wind did blow through this window last night?*

Just when Watson was about to raise this question, Teigen had already begun asking, "If this window were open last night during the shooting, then the person who shut the

window after the shooting must've been Mrs. Cubitt."

"That's right. Mr. Cubitt was shot to death after the first gunshot. A dead man couldn't have shut a window."

"But why must she shut the window?" asked the

shield (名) 屏障

baffled Teigen.

"The question that you should be asking first is, 'Why must she open the window?'"

"What?" Both Teigen and Watson were taken aback by Holmes's words.

open window ⟶ shut window

"A window must first be open for it to be shut later," said Holmes **matter-of- factly**. "Remember what Saunders told us earlier? In order to ward off intruders, Mr. Cubitt had ordered the maids to make sure all the windows and doors downstairs were shut before going to bed. However, Mrs. Cubitt had shut the window before attempting suicide, which means she must've opened the window beforehand. So the question we must ask is, 'Why did Mrs. Cubitt leave her bedroom in the middle of the night to go downstairs and open the window in the study?'"

"Hold on a second," objected Teigen. "We can only

matter-of-factly (副) 以事論事地

say for certain that Mrs. Cubitt was the one who shut the window. We can't be sure that she was also the person who opened the window."

"That's right," agreed Watson. "It could've been Mr. Cubitt who opened the window. Maybe he couldn't sleep so he went to the study to read. The weather was hot so he opened the window."

"Aha!" Holmes's sharp eyes switched from Watson to Teigen. "Your conjecture might've been plausible if there weren't a third gunshot."

Your conjecture might've been plausible if there weren't a third gunshot.

conjecture (名) 推測　plausible (形) 貌似合理的

91

The Third Gunshot

"A third gunshot? How was that possible? The two maids only heard two gunshots, not to mention that  the revolver found on the floor only had four bullets left inside, which meant only two shots were fired from the revolver," said the sceptical Teigen.

"Is that so?" said Holmes as he slowly stepped towards the window. He pointed his long, slender finger at a **wood knot** on the wall under the window frame and continued, "If only two shots were fired, then how do you explain this bullet?"

"What?" Taken aback by Holmes's discovery, Teigen quickly stepped towards the window and knelt down for a closer look. He took out a small knife and carefully dug the **blade** into the small black wood

slender (形) 瘦長的   wood knot (名) 木節疤   blade (名) 刀片

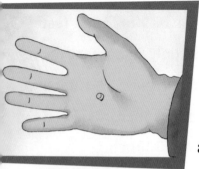

knot, "You are right! There is a bullet **buried** inside the wood knot!" Before Teigen had even finished his sentence, he had already *gouged* the bullet *out* of the wood knot.

Watson asked his old partner, "How did you notice the bullet? It was buried in such an **inconspicuous** spot!"

"That's because I was looking for it," said Holmes with a shrewd smile. "You were just looking around and not looking for anything specific. It's only natural that you would miss it."

Teigen pondered for a moment then said, "Including this bullet, there are three bullets found at the scene. So who fired the third gunshot?"

"That's a good question. We now know that there

---

buried (bury) (動) 埋藏　gouge(d) out (片語動) 挖出
inconspicuous (形) 不顯眼的

was one more gunshot, yet the revolver you found had fired just two gunshots. This could only mean that the third gunshot was fired from another gun. We must evaluate the situation again." Holmes then reviewed the details of the three gunshots as the following:

A The bullet that hit the wood knot:
Since the bullet was buried below the window frame inside the study, this gunshot was fired from the study towards the direction of the window. Therefore, this bullet should belong to the revolver found on the floor.

Bang

B The bullet that shot Mrs. Cubitt's left temple:
Not only was this gunshot fired from a close distance, remnants of gunpowder soot were found on Mrs. Cubitt's left hand and blood was found on the gun barrel, which could only mean that this gunshot was fired from the revolver found on the floor.

Left hand

C The bullet that shot Mr. Cubitt's heart:
Since both **A** and **B** were fired from the revolver found on the floor, this third bullet must've been fired from another gun.

evaluate (動) 估計、評估

"If my deduction were correct, then this means…" A frosty glimmer flashed across Holmes's eye before he continued, "Mrs. Cubitt wasn't the one who killed Mr. Cubitt. The killer was someone else!"

"But if there really were a gunshot C, how come the maids only heard the two gunshots A and B?" asked Teigen.

"The reason was simple. Gunshots A and C were fired at the same time. Saunders said that the first

gunshot was much louder than the second gunshot, which supported this theory," said Holmes. "The first loud bang was from the overlapping of gunshots A and C. The second softer bang was from gunshot B. That's

overlapping (形) 重疊的

why the maids only heard two gunshots."

"In that case, who shot Mr. Cubitt?" asked Teigen.

"The shooter must be our mystery man who drew the dancing stick figures!" suggested Watson *eagerly*.

"I think so too," said Holmes with a nod. "Mr. Cubitt said that he had seen a mystery man appear by the shed's front door. Mr. Cubitt had even spent long hours here and tried to **stake out** the mystery man. When I found out that the crime scene was right here in the study and gunshots were fired, I suspected right away that Mr. Cubitt and that mystery man had an *exchange* of *gunfire*."

"That's why you weren't *distracted* by the number of gunshot sounds at all. As soon as you stepped into the study, you went looking for evidence of gunfire exchange at once." Watson finally got the picture.

"Precisely. I quickly noticed the bullet hole in the wood knot below the window frame." Holmes looked over to Teigen before continuing, "Since a wood knot is itself a small hole, one could easily miss the bullet hole if one didn't look carefully. The

eagerly (副) 急切地　　stake out (片語動) 監視　　exchange of gunfire (名) 駁火、互相開槍
distract(ed) (動) 轉移注意力、分心、干擾

police missed it completely."

"Yes, we really did miss it." Despite his **embarrassment**, Teigen had no choice but to admit his men's **oversight** and feel impressed by Holmes.

"However, I had to first verify that the study's window was open during the shooting before I could verify the possibility of an exchange of gunfire, otherwise the window should've been broken from the shooting. That's why I went to see if the windows upstairs were open to allow air convection. If air was moving, the maids should be able to smell gunpowder odour before they went downstairs."

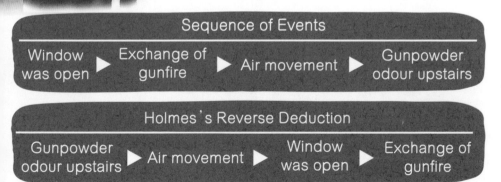

Sequence of Events			
Window was open ▶	Exchange of gunfire ▶	Air movement ▶	Gunpowder odour upstairs

Holmes's Reverse Deduction			
Gunpowder odour upstairs ▶	Air movement ▶	Window was open ▶	Exchange of gunfire

embarrassment (名) 尷尬   oversight (名) 疏忽

"I see. No wonder you asked the maids about odours in such detail," said Watson.

"Once I've confirmed that they could smell gunpowder odour upstairs, I was sure that the study's window was open," said Holmes. "I'm guessing that Mrs. Cubitt contacted the mystery man behind Mr. Cubitt's back in an attempt to settle the **treacherous** situation herself. They were to meet by the study's window at 3 a.m., upon which she was going to pay him to leave her and her husband alone for good. The US$500 in the manila envelope is material evidence."

treacherous (形) 危險的

"But Mr. Cubitt had walked into their late night meeting unexpectedly, resulting in an exchange of gunfire," further deduced Teigen.

"Yes, and they both opened fire at the same time. Unfortunately, Mr. Cubitt got shot and died, but the bullet he fired didn't hit the mystery man and hit the wood knot below the window frame instead."

"I see." Watson understood at last.

"Since the deal had *gone sour*, the mystery man *fled* the scene immediately. Mrs. Cubitt was worried that he might change his mind and turn back, so she closed the window right away. Once she realised that her husband was dead, she was so **devastated** that she turned the gun to herself."

"That makes

gone (go) sour (片語) 出了差錯　fled (flee) (動) 逃離
devastated (形) 極度悲痛的、大受打擊的

99

sense," agreed Teigen. "Unfortunately, Mrs. Cubitt is still unconscious so we can't ask her where we could find the mystery man."

 "No need to ask her. I know where he is."

"What? How do you know?"

 "The mystery man told me."

"How is that possible? This is no time for jokes, you know."

 "I'm not joking. Don't you remember? I can decipher the dancing stick figure drawings."

"Those drawings disclosed his whereabouts ?"

 "They certainly did. According to the drawings, his name is Abe Slaney."

"Abe Slaney?"

unconscious (形) 昏迷不醒的   whereabouts (名) 行蹤

"Yes. The telegram I sent to the New York police earlier was a request to investigate the relationship between Abe Slaney and Elsie. The reply was filled with rather surprising information," said Holmes. "It turns out that Elsie is from New York's Chinatown and her father was the notorious Iron Crutch Lee, who started a kung fu school as a front to mask the activities of his gang called Blue Dragons. Abe Slaney is one of the ringleaders of Blue Dragons. His left forearm has a nasty scar that's shaped like a lightning rod, so Abe Slaney also bears the nickname Lightning Abe. Iron Crutch Lee died from illness about a year ago and Elsie disappeared soon after her father's funeral. Two months later, conflicts within the gang sprang up as various parties fought for the seat of head boss. The

---

notorious (形) 惡名昭彰的、臭名遠播的　crutch (名) 拐杖
ringleader(s) (名) 頭目、首領　nasty scar (形+名) 可怕的疤痕
sprang (spring) up (片語動) 湧現、突然出現

police have been hunting down Abe Slaney after he killed several members of his own gang."

"No wonder Elsie has refused to talk about her past," said Watson.

"About a month ago, the New York police received a lead that Abe Slaney had board a steamship and fled to Hong Kong. It's likely that he is **lodging** at a local kung

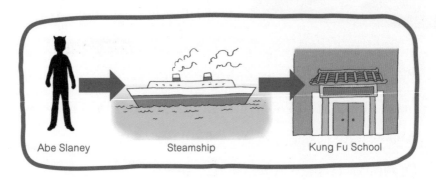

| Abe Slaney | Steamship | Kung Fu School |

fu school," said Holmes. "But what I don't understand is, Abe Slaney's stick figure drawings indicated that he was on a steamship called Argyle, but the sailing schedules on the newspaper said this British steamship is not docked at the port of Hong Kong right now."

"That is strange," said Watson.

"What's even stranger was that the stick figure

lodging (lodge) (動) 借宿

message spelled out 'AT ARGYLE'. If he were on the steamship, shouldn't it be 'ON' instead of 'AT'? An American wouldn't make such an elementary preposition error."

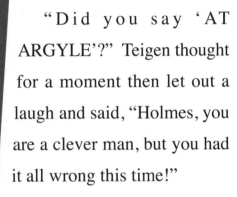

"Did you say 'AT ARGYLE'?" Teigen thought for a moment then let out a laugh and said, "Holmes, you are a clever man, but you had it all wrong this time!"

"What did I have wrong?"

"It is true that ARGYLE is a British steamship that sails between India and South China, but ARGYLE is also the name of a street in Hong Kong."

"Are you serious?" Holmes was utterly surprised.

"Argyle Street is on Kowloon side in an area called Mongkok."

"I see! In that case, he must be hiding in a kung fu school on Argyle Street."

"Kung fu school? Can we trust that the information obtained from the New York police is accurate?" asked Teigen.

"I believe it should be accurate," said Holmes. "I remember Mr. Cubitt once said that his wife became very frightened when she saw someone practicing kung fu at the Peak Garden. Perhaps that kung fu practitioner was actually a messenger and he was using his kung fu poses to convey a message, same as the secret code in the dancing stick figure drawings."

"Oh, I understand now!" cried Watson. "The stick figure drawings look like kung fu poses!"

"Yes. When the New York police mentioned kung fu school in the telegram, I immediately made the connection in my head. A kung fu school is a place full of kung fu practitioners, so finding a practitioner who is willing to learn a few poses then perform those moves in front of Elsie shouldn't have taken much effort."

"That particular kung fu school must be on Argyle Street!" said Watson.

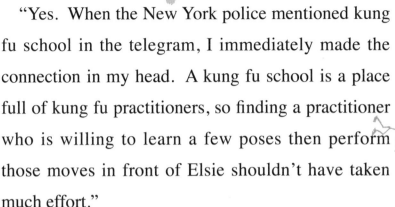

"I will **assemble** a few teams of police officers to search the kung fu schools in that area. We should be able to find Abe Slaney in no time," said Teigen as he rubbed his fists in **anticipation**.

"I don't think that's a good idea," disagreed Holmes. "We don't want to set off any alarm. Not

assemble (動) 召集　　anticipation (名) 期待

to mention that Abe Slaney has a gun. We don't want anyone to get hurt."

"What should we do then?" asked Watson.

"Let's go to Argyle Street first and see how many kung fu schools there are. If there aren't that many, we should be able to investigate quietly and locate Abe Slaney easily," suggested Holmes.

"I'm good with that suggestion," agreed Teigen. "It's less trouble for me if we could catch him without causing a **commotion**."

commotion (名) 混亂、騷亂

Luring out the Villain

   In order not to draw attention, Teigen changed out of his uniform and put on his own clothes before taking Holmes and Watson to Argyle Street. A quick inquiry at the district police station told them that Argyle Street had four kung fu schools.

Pretending to be tourists, the three men went to the four kung fu schools and circled around the outside of each school. Holmes asked Watson and Teigen, "Do you remember smelling a ***distinct*** odour when we passed by the front door of the third kung fu school?"

"Was there an odour?" Teigen shook his head and said, "I was so focused on the people walking in and out of the school that I hadn't noticed any odour."

"Me neither. Did that odour seem dubious?" asked Watson.

"I can't say for sure but that odour smells familiar..." said Holmes as he furrowed his eyebrows and thought hard.

"Are you telling me that you can't tell what kind of

distinct (形) 獨特的　　dubious (形) 可疑的

odour that was at the third school? You're usually so sensitive with smells that you could recognise the brand of someone's cigar after just one whiff. Have you lost your gift?" teased Watson at Holmes.

"Hmmm... That was an odour that I'm not accustomed to, though I think I might have smelled it recently. What could it possibly..." A glimmer suddenly flashed across Holmes's eye, "I remember now! It was the same odour that I smelled on the paper aeroplane!"

Holmes pulled from his pocket the paper aeroplane that Cubitt had delivered to their hotel earlier. Holmes placed the plane in front of his nose and sniffed hard, "Yes, this is it! The third kung fu school smells exactly the same as this paper aeroplane!"

Teigen leaned over for a sniff and recognised the scent right away, "This is the scent of brewing traditional Chinese herbal medicines . When I first came to Hong Kong, I investigated a murder that happened at a

whiff (名) 聞一聞、嗅一嗅　accustom(ed) to (片語動) 熟悉
Chinese herbal medicine(s) (名) 中藥

109

traditional Chinese medicine clinic. This odour was seeping at every corner of that clinic."

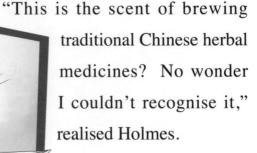

"This is the scent of brewing traditional Chinese herbal medicines? No wonder I couldn't recognise it," realised Holmes.

"Why would a kung fu school carry this odour?" asked Watson.

"Kung fu schools in Hong Kong are different from our gyms back home. Many kung fu schools also offer Chinese chiropractic treatments. Some kung fu schoolmasters are traditional Chinese medicine practitioners themselves. They see patients and brew herbal medicines for the patients," said Teigen. "It's possible that the third kung fu school we passed by is also a traditional Chinese medicine clinic."

"I see. The scent of brewing traditional Chinese herbal medicines must have infused into the paper aeroplane, just like receipts from Indian restaurants

Chinese chiropractic treatment(s) (名) 跌打治療　infuse(d) (動) 滲入

always carry an aroma of curry." Holmes paused for a second as a sharp glimmer flashed across his eye, "Without a doubt, that kung fu school is where Abe Slaney is hiding!"

"Brilliant! Now that we know where he is, we shall go catch him right away!" said the excited Teigen.

"Slow down for a second," **dissuaded** Holmes.

"Let's not forget that his hiding place is a kung fu school, which means everyone inside is trained in martial arts. We would be met by strong **resistance** if we were to just storm in, and Abe Slaney might slip away in the midst of confusion."

aroma (名) 香味   dissuade(d) (動) 勸阻   resistance (名) 反抗

"You're right. What do you suggest we do then?"

"I'll write him a note and ask him to come out."

"What?" exclaimed Watson and Teigen in disbelief.

"Don't you remember? I've mastered the stick figure code," said Holmes. "Abe Slaney fired a gunshot in the dark last night and he didn't even take the money before he fled. His *hastened* departure means that he probably isn't aware of Elsie's suicide attempt. If I were to send him a stick figure message in Elsie's name, he would definitely come out of the kung fu school to meet with her. Once he is out on the street, we can do whatever we want."

"That's a clever plan!" praised Teigen. The three men then went into a nearby restaurant and pretended to sit down for a meal. Holmes asked to borrow a sheet of paper and drew 14 stick figures on the paper. He then gave a few dollars to a waiter and asked him to deliver the note to the kung fu school.

hastened (形) 急忙的、匆匆的

"Remember to say that the message is

from Miss Elsie," instructed Holmes to the waiter.

As soon as the waiter stepped out of the restaurant, the three men followed behind the waiter until he reached the kung fu school and handed the note to someone at the school. The three men then hid behind a corner of a nearby dark alley in wait for Slaney to come out from the school.

Sure enough, less than 10 minutes after the message reached the kung fu school, a muscular middle-aged man quickly stepped out of the school.

Holmes gave a signalling glance to Watson and Teigen then quietly walked up to the middle-

muscular (形) 滿身肌肉的、身形魁梧的

113

aged man from behind and put his hand on the man's shoulder, "Abe Slaney! Aren't you supposed to be in New York? What are you doing here?"

The startled man quickly turned around.

"Abe! It's me! Remember me?" said Holmes with a big smile on his face. "We had dinner once at a restaurant in Chinatown, New York. That must be two years ago. Iron Crutch Lee introduced you to me. Have you forgotten already?"

The man seemed puzzled for a moment then said crossly, "You got the wrong man."

"I don't think so." Holmes took a step forward then pressed down his voice and said, "I know that the New York police is looking for you. But don't worry. We're both players of the underworld. I won't sell you out."

The man's eyes were filled with **aggravation** upon hearing those words. He **gritted** his

teeth and **growled** at Holmes in a low

voice, "I said you got the wrong man.

I don't have time for your nonsense."

"Have I really got the wrong man?

I don't think so." Holmes

pointed at the nasty scar

on the man's left

forearm and said with an

icy chuckle, "I might not know

your face but I can identify that

scar for sure. Where is the

message that Elsie wrote you?

---

crossly (副) 生氣地　　aggravation (名) 不耐煩、惱怒
grit(ted) one's teeth (習) 咬牙切齒　　growl(ed) (動) 怒吼着

Or should I say, where is the message that I wrote you? Is it in your pocket, Mr. Lightning Abe?"

"What?" The surprised Slaney quickly reached his hand to his waist.

In the blink of an eye, Teigen was already standing

behind Slaney. With his gun pointing at the back of Slaney's head, Teigen shouted, "Don't move or I'll shoot!" Slaney froze upon hearing Teigen's words and Holmes quickly confiscated the gun that was tucked in Slaney's waistband.

in the blink of an eye (習) 瞬間　　confiscate(d) (動) 沒收
tuck(ed) (動) 夾着、塞進

Decoding the Message of the Stick Figures

When Slaney was taken to the police station's questioning room, he had refused to admit to any *wrongdoing* at first. However, after the coroner pulled the bullet out of Cubitt's body and found the **markings** on the bullet matched with Slaney's gun, Slaney had no choice but to tell the truth.

It turned out that Slaney was an **orphan**. He was brought up by Iron Crutch Lee and he grew up together with Elsie in Chinatown, New York. Before he passed away, Iron Crutch Lee had wanted Elsie to marry Slaney, but Elsie refused because she had always thought of Slaney as her brother and had no romantic feelings towards him. Then after

wrongdoing (名) 違法行為   coroner (名) 驗屍官
marking(s) (名) 槍膛線的痕跡、標記   orphan (名) 孤兒

Iron Crutch Lee's death, Elsie ran away from home, hoping to free herself from the mobster family that she so despised and break away from Slaney's pestering pursuit once and for all.

Soon after Elsie left home, Slaney killed a few members of his own gang and was wanted by the police. While he was on the run, he found out that Elsie had gone to Hong Kong, so he wrote her a letter to tell her that he was heading to Hong Kong to bring her back home and make her his wife. One month later, he made his way to Hong Kong as a stowaway. Even though he was thousands of miles away from New York, he was still a wanted criminal. He needed to be inconspicuous and not attract any attention, so he sent messages to Elsie in the stick figure codes that were regularly used for secret communication within the gang. Apparently, Iron Crutch Lee was inspired by kung fu manuals when he came up with this secret coding system.

Elsie was unwavering in her refusal to meet with Slaney. She even replied him with a stick figure drawing on the wall of the shed that spelled out the word 'NEVER'.

mobster family (名) 黑幫家族　　pestering (名) 糾纏、滋擾　　stowaway (名) 偷渡者
unwavering (形) 毫不動搖的

Filled with anger upon seeing her message, Slaney tossed a paper aeroplane to her garden with a final warning message written inside. What happened  after was just as Holmes had deduced. Elsie sent a message back to Slaney, instructing him to meet her by the study's window at 3 a.m., telling him that she would give him US$500 in return for her freedom from her former life.

The study's window was open when Slaney arrived at the garden. He could see Elsie standing inside the house. Just when he was about to reach for the money, a black shadow suddenly appeared and fired a gunshot

at him, but he was quick enough to pull out his gun right away and shoot at the shadow too.

"Gunshots fired in the middle of the night were

especially loud, so I had to flee the scene at once. I have no idea that I've killed a man, and I certainly have no clue that Elsie would turn the gun to herself. If I had known this would happen, I wouldn't have come over to find her," said Slaney regretfully.

"It's too late for remorse now," said Teigen coldly. "Prepare to suffer for your own sins."

Holmes and Watson stepped out of the questioning room after the truth was revealed. However, Watson still did not understand how Holmes managed to crack the stick figure code.

"Cracking the code wasn't that complicated, actually," said Holmes. "Once I realised that each stick figure stood for a letter of the English alphabet, deciphering the messages became pretty straightforward."

"Really? But you still needed to figure out which stick figure stood for which particular letter. The difficulty

remorse (名) 懊悔、自責

in that task is **unthinkable** to me."

"It's not that difficult if you know about the pattern of letters in words. In English, the letter E appears most frequently, even in short phrases. When I saw the first drawing of 15 stick figures, I noticed that four of the stick figures looked exactly the same, so I thought the repeating stick figure was very likely representing the letter E," explained Holmes. "Moreover, words in written English are separated by spaces, so I had to look for a symbol that represented a separator. Within the 15 stick figures, I noticed that three of them were drawn with one hand holding a handkerchief. That handkerchief was obviously meant as a separator. From that, I knew that this drawing of 15 stick figures was actually a phrase with four words."

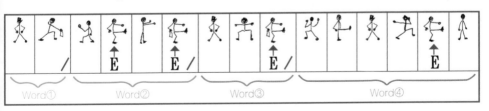

unthinkable (形) 難以想像的

"That makes sense," said Watson. "Then how did you decode the other stick figures?"

"Letters used repeatedly in English in the order of frequency are T, A, O, I, N, S, H, R, D, L. But since the usage frequency of T, A, O, I are pretty much the same, I couldn't decode properly without more samples of drawings."

"That's why you asked Cubitt to bring you more drawings."

"Yes," said Holmes. "When he came to see us the second time, he brought over three more strips of paper. Two strips appeared to be short phrases. The remaining strip had only one word of five stick figures where two of the stick figures representing the letter E were the second and fourth letter of the word."

"A five-letter word with two E's as the second and fourth letter?" Watson thought for a moment then continued, "The most common words that I could think of are 'SEVER', 'LEVER' and 'NEVER'."

"Exactly," said Holmes. "In my analysis earlier, I had determined that this word must be Elsie's resolute reply to her intimidator, which led me to conclude that this stick figure drawing most likely spelled out 'NEVER'. With that, I was able to connect which stick figures stood for N, V and R."

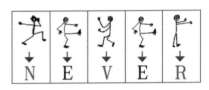

"By then, you had already matched four stick figures to four letters, E, N, V, R."

"Yes, but that still wasn't enough," said Holmes. "I speculated; that if the sender and receiver knew each other, their names would probably be mentioned in the messages. So the next thing I did was try to look for Elsie's name in the drawings. It was easier than I had expected, because I quickly found her name in the second paper strip."

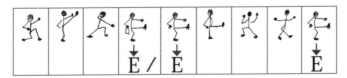

speculate(d) (動) 推測

"Oh, I get it!" said Watson. "The second word in that message was a five-letter word beginning and ending with the letter E, which matched Elsie's name."

"Upon finding Elsie's name, I started to examine the letters in the first word of that message," said Holmes. "I had already determined that the mysterious sender must be an intimidator, so the word in the message before Elsie's name must be some sort of command. Since the word ended with the letter E, I made a guess that it could likely be the word 'COME'."

"That's brilliant!" praised Watson. "In addition to E, N, V, R, you had now also found the six stick figures that matched with the letters L, S, I, C, O, M!"

"Then I went back to the first drawing," said Holmes. "Besides the letter E, I could now fill in the letters, M, R, S, L and N."

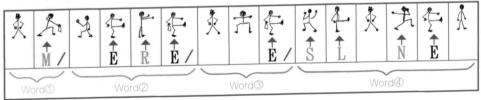

"The second word was '_ERE'. That could be the word 'HERE'," said Watson.

"That was my exact thought," said Holmes. "Moreover, the first word was a two-letter word ending with M. The answer was obviously 'AM'. I now knew that particular stick figure stood for A, and I was lucky to find the same stick figure repeating twice in that same message."

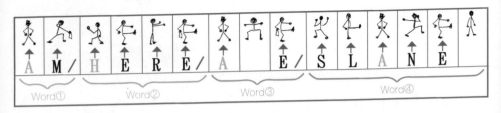

"'A_E' and 'SLANE_'? That had to be 'ABE SLANEY'!" The name rolled out of Watson's tongue without giving much thought.

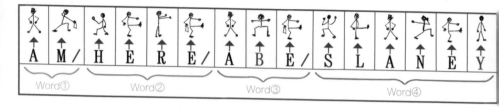

"Yes. The most common English given name and surname that would fit the blank spaces would be 'ABE SLANEY'," said Holmes. "That's why I sent the name to the New York police via telegram right away to see if they had heard of him. It turned out Abe Slaney was wanted by the New York police so they replied me with information on his background."

"I see."

"Besides the ten letters E, N, V, R, L, S, I, C, O, M, the stick figures that matched with the letters A, H, B, Y were also decoded at that point. With so many letters on hand, I was able to spell out the message on the remaining paper strip."

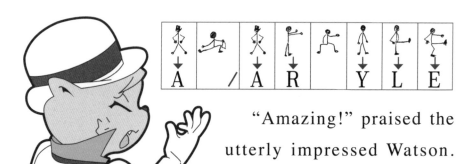

"Amazing!" praised the utterly impressed Watson. "You started with only one stick figure representing the letter E, and through a tenacious process of deduction, you were able to decode all the messages! How amazing was that?"

"It wasn't that amazing," said Holmes as he waved his hand in nonchalance. "Remember how I figured out that you had decided not to invest in the South African mines just by noticing the chalk on the left hand between your thumb and index finger? The two deduction processes were pretty much the same. I might have started with just one clue, but through considering other known information and deducing step by step, drawing to a logical conclusion wasn't difficult at all. What appeared to be complicated was actually rather straightforward."

tenacious (形) 鍥而不捨的　　nonchalance (名) 若無其事

"You made it sound so simple. I, for one, don't think I can do it."

"Even though the case is solved and the killer is caught, it's most unfortunate that I couldn't crack the code in time to prevent this tragedy from happening," said Holmes as he let out a deep sigh. "I'm so sorry that you've lost a good friend, Watson."

"Yes…" muttered Watson sadly. "And Elsie is still in a coma. God only knows when she would wake up…"

tragedy (名) 悲劇　coma (名) 昏迷狀態